FINAL YEARS
OF THE
AMERICAN
REVOLUTION

BY JOHN HAMILTON

VISIT US AT
WWW.ABDOPUBLISHING.COM

Published by ABDO Publishing Company, PO Box 398166, Minneapolis, MN 55439.
Copyright ©2013 by Abdo Consulting Group, Inc. International copyrights reserved in all countries. No part of this book may be reproduced in any form without written permission from the publisher. ABDO & Daughters™ is a trademark and logo of ABDO Publishing Company.

Printed in the United States of America, North Mankato, Minnesota.
122012
012013

 PRINTED ON RECYCLED PAPER

Editor: Sue Hamilton
Graphic Design: Sue Hamilton
Cover Design: Neil Klinepier
Cover: Painting by Don Troiani, www.historicalartprints.com
Interior Photos and Illustrations: AP-pgs 1, 7, 20, 21, 22 & 25; Architect of the Capitol-pgs 23 & 27; Granger Collection-pgs 4, 9, 16, 19 & 24; John Hamilton-pgs 6 & 18; Military and Historical Image Bank-pgs 11, 12-13, 17 & 29; iStockphoto-pg 28; Library of Congress-pg 26; National Archives-pg 15; U.S. Army Center of Military History-pgs 3 & 5.

ABDO Booklinks
To learn more about the American Revolution, visit ABDO Publishing Company online. Web sites about the American Revolution are featured on our Book Links pages. These links are routinely monitored and updated to provide the most current information available.
Web site: www.abdopublishing.com

Library of Congress Control Number: 2012945997

Cataloging-in-Publication Data

Hamilton, John.
 Final years of the American Revolution / John Hamilton.
   p. cm. -- (American Revolution)
Includes index.
ISBN 978-1-61783-680-0
1. United States--History--Revolution, 1775-1783--Campaigns--Juvenile literature. 2. United States--History--Revolution, 1775-1783--Peace--Juvenile literature.   I. Title.
973.3/3--dc22

                                    2012945997

CONTENTS

War On The Frontier

Throughout the American Revolution, there was continuous violence on the western frontier, in wilderness areas ranging from New York to Georgia. Native Americans were alarmed at white settlers taking over their lands. During the war, they often sided with Great Britain, convinced by promises from King George III's representatives that Native American land rights would be respected. Famous Iroquois leader Joseph Brant fought for the British, along with thousands of his people.

British officials encouraged Native Americans and British Loyalists to raid white settlements.

The attacks resulted in terror and destruction. Some of the worst-hit areas were in Pennsylvania's Wyoming Valley and New York's Mohawk Valley. In 1778, hundreds of settlers were killed, and many towns were torched. Revenge attacks by settlers against Native Americans killed many more.

News of the massacres in New York and Pennsylvania infuriated Americans. George Washington sent Major General John Sullivan on an expedition to crush the Iroquois threat. In southwestern New York, at the Battle of Newtown, Sullivan's force of 4,000 soldiers defeated about 1,100 Iroquois and Loyalists on August 29, 1779.

4

George Rogers Clark takes the British stronghold at Vincennes in 1779.

Afterwards, Sullivan's army roamed northward, destroying Iroquois villages and crops. That winter, many Iroquois starved, or fled to Canada. However, the very next year, raids on settlements continued.

General George Rogers Clark was a frontiersman from Virginia. He commanded Patriot militia troops in the wilderness areas of the northwestern frontier. He captured key British strongholds, including Kaskaskia (in today's Illinois), and Vincennes (in Indiana). This reduced Native American attacks, but violence between white settlers and Native Americans would continue to erupt for decades after the war.

WAR IN THE SOUTH

Great Britain suffered a crushing defeat at the Battle of Saratoga in October 1777. With France entering the war on the side of the Patriots, Great Britain shifted its efforts to the Southern colonies. King George III hoped that many British Loyalists would rise up to support the mother country. Once the Southern colonies were under control, the British could then push north to renew attacks on the Northern colonies.

In December 1778, the British captured the river port town of Savannah, Georgia. In the fall of 1779, a combined force of American troops and French warships tried to retake the town. The attack was a dismal failure, with over 1,000 French and American troops killed, wounded, or captured.

The following spring, in April and May 1780, British forces attacked and captured Charleston, South Carolina.

It was one of the most disastrous American defeats of the entire war. The Patriots lost 89 killed, 138 wounded, and 6,684 captured. The British also captured more than 150 cannons, tons of gunpowder, and food for their troops.

The British captured the river port town of Savannah, Georgia, in December 1778. In the fall of 1779, a combined force of American troops and French warships tried to retake the town. The attack was a dismal failure for the Patriots.

After the fall of Charleston, South Carolina, General Charles Cornwallis took command of the British forces in the Southern colonies. His orders were to conquer North and South Carolina, and then push north into Virginia.

American Patriot and British Loyalist militias continued to battle in the Southern colonies. Fighting was especially intense in the wilderness areas of Georgia, with both sides sometimes committing atrocities against innocent people. Patriot morale began to waver in the face of such terrible losses. The British plan so far seemed to be working.

The Battle of Camden

After the crushing loss of Charleston, South Carolina, the Continental Congress sent General Horatio Gates to take command of the Patriot southern army. Gates was in command when the Americans won at Saratoga, New York, in 1777. He arrived in North Carolina in July 1780. After gathering approximately 900 Continental Army soldiers and 2,800 inexperienced, poorly equipped militia troops, he marched south into South Carolina.

Gates's destination was Camden, a crossroads town used by the British as an arms depot. The long journey over difficult terrain was hot and miserable. Many of the hungry and thirsty men suffered heat stroke.

On August 16, 1780, Gates's men met a large force of battle-hardened

General Horatio Gates

Redcoats commanded by General Charles Cornwallis. Cornwallis had learned of Gates's expedition and had moved up from Charleston to stop the rebel army.

Both sides set up their forces on either side of a road running just north of Camden. Gates foolishly positioned his least experienced

The Continental Army suffered terrible losses at the hands of the experienced British Army at the Battle of Camden, South Carolina, on August 16, 1780.

militiamen opposite Cornwallis's finest troops. When the Redcoats advanced, the militiamen panicked and fled. The Patriot Continental soldiers put up a spirited fight, but soon they, too, were forced to retreat or surrender. At the end of the battle, the Americans lost about 250 men killed and 800 wounded or captured.

After the terrible loss at Camden, what was left of the Continental Army limped back to North Carolina. The incompetent General Gates was replaced by General Nathanael Greene, one of George Washington's most trusted officers. Greene immediately began the task of rebuilding the southern army and propping up its sagging morale.

October 7, 1780

The Battle Of Kings Mountain

As General Charles Cornwallis's army marched north toward Charlotte, North Carolina, its left side was protected by a unit of Loyalist militiamen commanded by Major Patrick Ferguson. Ferguson's troops roamed the countryside, hunting down and punishing disloyal rebels. He sent word to Patriots in the area, saying that he would "march his army over the mountains, hang their leaders, and lay their country waste with fire and sword."

On October 7, 1780, Ferguson's 1,075 Loyalist troops were intercepted by 910 Patriot militiamen. The rebels encircled the Loyalists, who had set up defensive positions on a tall ridge known as Kings Mountain, South Carolina, near the border with North Carolina.

The Patriots, most of them rugged frontiersmen, twice charged up the steep, rocky ridge, only to be driven back by Loyalist sharpshooters. Ferguson dashed from place to place along the ridge on horseback, directing his men. Suddenly, he fell from his horse, fatally wounded by Patriot musket fire. The surviving Loyalists, running out of ammunition and facing continued Patriot bayonet charges, surrendered.

British Loyalist leader Major Patrick Ferguson is killed by Patriot militiamen.

However, some Patriot militiamen did not want to take prisoners, and the killing continued until rebel officers gained control of the situation.

The Americans lost 29 men killed and 59 wounded. For the British Loyalists, the battle was a total disaster: 244 killed, 163 wounded, and 668 captured. The surprising loss stunned General Cornwallis, who delayed his invasion of North Carolina for several months. This gave the Patriot forces much-needed time to gain strength in men and supplies. In addition to boosting Patriot confidence, the battle also shattered the morale of Loyalists. The British plan of riding a wave of Loyalist support in the war was finished.

The Battle Of Cowpens

By early 1781, General Nathanael Greene was busy rebuilding the Continental Army's southern forces. Lacking the manpower to directly challenge the enemy, Greene sent General Daniel Morgan and about 1,065 men to harass British forces in South Carolina. Morgan was skilled in guerrilla warfare, and well respected by his men.

When British General Charles Cornwallis learned of Morgan's mission, he sent Colonel Banastre "Bloody Ban" Tarleton to stop the Americans. Tarleton was hated by the Patriots because of his reputation for killing soldiers even after they had surrendered.

Tarleton pursued Morgan to a place near the South Carolina and North Carolina border called "Hannah's Cowpens," which was a pasture ground for livestock. It was an ideal place for Morgan to spring a trap on Tarleton's troops. On January 17, 1781, the two sides clashed.

When the Redcoats advanced, lines of American militia opened fire, while Continental Army riflemen and cavalry attacked from the sides. The British were caught in a killing zone. Patriot bayonet charges forced the Redcoat infantry to flee or surrender. Tarleton counterattacked with a cavalry charge. Each side furiously slashed at each other with sabers, but the British finally fled the field of battle.

The British lost 110 men killed, 200 wounded, and 529 captured at the Battle of Cowpens. The Patriots suffered 60 wounded and only 12 killed. American morale soared with yet another decisive victory.

Patriot troops overrun a British unit at the Battle of Cowpens.

THE ARTICLES OF CONFEDERATION

A constitution is a set of laws and ideas that spell out how a nation is governed. The first constitution of the United States was called the Articles of Confederation and Perpetual Union. It was an agreement between the 13 original colonies that loosely tied them together into one republic. (A republic is a nation in which power is held by citizens and their elected representatives, with a president as head of the government instead of a king or queen.)

The Articles of Confederation were written by a committee of politicians headed by John Dickinson of Pennsylvania. The document was presented to the Continental Congress on July 12, 1776. After 16 months of debate, Congress sent a highly modified version to the states for approval on November 15, 1777. The states squabbled and debated and negotiated for years, but finally, on March 1, 1781, the Articles of Confederation were approved, or "ratified."

The nation's new constitution gave most political power to the individual states. Americans were afraid of creating a strong central government like Great Britain's, which might lead to more oppression. The Articles of Confederation set up a national congress of lawmakers. Each state, no matter how many people lived there, had one vote. Nine out of 13 states had to approve actions such as raising a military force or borrowing money.

The Articles of Confederation held the country together during the war years, even before they were officially ratified. But the central government was too weak to truly unite the states. A political solution would have to be found, but first the war needed to be won.

ARTICLES

OF

CONFEDERATION AND PERPETUAL UNION,

BETWEEN THE STATES OF

1777
Monday April 21

NEW-HAMPSHIRE,	~~THE COUNTIES OF NEW-CASTLE KENT AND SUSSEX of~~ DELAWARE,
MASSACHUSETTS-BAY,	
RHODE-ISLAND,	MARYLAND,
CONNECTICUT,	VIRGINIA,
NEW-YORK,	NORTH-CAROLINA,
NEW-JERSEY,	SOUTH-CAROLINA, AND
PENNSYLVANIA,	GEORGIA.

april 25

Art. 2 Each state retains its so-
vereignty, freedom & independence
and every power jurisdiction and
right, which is not by this confederation
expressly delegated to the united states
in Congress assembled.
agreed

Art 3. Agreed to.

ART. I. THE name of this Confederacy shall be "THE UNITED STATES OF AMERICA."

ART. ~~II.~~ *3* The said States hereby severally enter into a firm league of friendship with each other, for their common defence, the security of their liberties, and their mutual and general welfare, binding themselves to assist each other against all force offered to or attacks made upon them or any of them, on account of religion, sovereignty, trade, or any other pretence whatever.

ART. III. Each State reserves to itself the sole and exclusive regulation and government of its internal police in all matters that shall not interfere with the articles of this Confederation.

Agreed
21 Octo 1777

ART. IV. No State, without the consent of the United States in Congress Assembled, shall send any Embassy to or receive any embassy from, or enter into any conference, agreement, alliance or treaty with any King, Prince or State; nor shall any person holding any office of profit or trust under the United States or any them, accept of any present, emolument, office or title of any kind whatever from any King, Prince or foreign State; nor shall the United States Assembled, or any of them, grant any title of nobility.

agreed
21 Octr. 1777.

ART. V. No two or more States shall enter into any treaty, confederation or alliance whatever between them without the consent of the United States in Congress Assembled, specifying accurately the purposes for which the same is to be entered into, and how long it shall continue.

agreed
Sept 23 1777

ART. VI. No State shall lay any imposts or duties which may interfere with any stipulations in treaties ~~hereafter~~ entered into by the United States Assembled with any King, Prince or State. *in pursuance of any treaties already proposed by Congress to the courts of France and Spain*

A printed and corrected copy of page one of the Articles of Confederation, modified by the Continental Congress in 1777.

THE BATTLE OF GUILFORD COURTHOUSE

After the humiliating British defeat at the Battle of Cowpens, General Charles Cornwallis wanted revenge. His 2,100-man army pursued Nathanael Greene's Patriots in a cat-and-mouse chase across North Carolina. Greene refused to engage the Redcoats while his rebel army was still weak. He retreated across the Dan River into Virginia and then set up camp to rest and gather new recruits.

General Charles Cornwallis

By March 14, 1781, Greene's resupplied army had grown to 4,500 troops. He crossed back into North Carolina, ready to fight the Redcoats.

The two sides clashed on March 15, 1781, at a rural county seat called Guilford Courthouse. The courthouse itself rested on the north side of the battlefield. Greene set up three lines of troops on the cold, rain-soaked fields and awaited a British attack.

General Cornwallis ordered his men to charge forward. The Redcoats were seasoned veterans, but they were struck by withering Patriot musket fire. Many officers were cut down. A rebel cavalry charge almost destroyed a British battalion, but Cornwallis directed his artillery to fire grapeshot into the melee.

Patriot cavalry charges a British battalion during the Battle of Guilford Courthouse.

The attack stopped, but the cannons killed both rebels and Redcoats.

At the end of about two hours of battle, Greene ordered his troops to retreat. Cornwallis won the battle, but the price was terribly high: the British lost more than 25 percent of their officers and troops. Total casualties included 93 British killed and 413 wounded. The Americans lost 70 killed and 185 wounded.

After the battle, Greene turned his army south. Over the next several months, in a series of battles, he unraveled British control of the Southern colonies.

Cornwallis and his troops were now weak and poorly supplied. The British limped across the border into Virginia, setting the stage for the last big battle of the American Revolution.

September 28—October 19, 1781

THE SIEGE OF YORKTOWN

After the Battle of Guilford Courthouse in North Carolina on March 15, 1781, British General Charles Cornwallis moved his battered army north into Virginia. He eventually united with other British forces, including a group of Redcoats and Loyalists commanded by the traitor General Benedict Arnold. The once-proud Patriot Arnold had been roaming the countryside, burning and pillaging the towns and villages of his fellow Americans.

In British-occupied New York City, General Henry Clinton, commander of all British forces in North America, was growing frightened of an American attack on the city. Patriot General George Washington had recently joined forces with a French army commanded by General Comte de Rochambeau. The combined armies were camped north of New York City, threatening attack.

Clinton sent a confusing set of instructions to General Cornwallis in Virginia. At first, Clinton wanted Cornwallis to move his forces north to reinforce New York City. Then he changed his mind and ordered Cornwallis to build a defensible port at Yorktown, Virginia.

VIRGINIA

York River

Yorktown

Chesapeake Bay

James River

N

- American and French Armies
- British Army
- French Navy

George Washington surveys the battlefield at Yorktown, Virginia.

The mighty British Royal Navy, the general hoped, would be able to resupply Cornwallis's troops with food and weapons, or quickly transport them to New York City if needed.

Cornwallis arrived in Yorktown by August 1781 and began setting up a defensive network of redoubts and earthworks to defend his force of about 7,200 soldiers.

When George Washington learned that Cornwallis had moved his entire army to the narrow peninsula at Yorktown, he knew the British general had made a grave error. If the Patriots could seal off the peninsula and somehow keep British ships from resupplying their army, Washington could lay siege to the Redcoats and slowly crush them. Washington and French commander Comte de Rochambeau quickly moved the bulk of their armies south to Virginia. The allies had a combined force of about 17,600 soldiers, which included 9,000 Americans and 8,600 French troops.

On September 5, 1781, a French fleet of ships under the command of Admiral Comte de Grasse sailed to the mouth of Chesapeake Bay. The French fought a sea battle against Royal Navy ships commanded by British Admiral Thomas Graves. The two sides lined up against each other, so close they were nearly within pistol range. Then they pummeled each other with fiery cannons.

The superior British ships had difficulty communicating with each other, and missed opportunities to destroy the French. At the end of the day, seven Royal Navy ships were badly damaged, with several hundred sailors killed or wounded. The British fleet limped back to New York City, while the French set up a naval blockade around Yorktown.

Comte de Rochambeau meets Washington.

The British frigate *Sharon* burns
during the Battle of Yorktown, 1781.

If the French had not won the naval battle that day, General Cornwallis would have received fresh troops and supplies. The war might have been won by the British. Instead, with the French victory, the noose was tightening by the day around Cornwallis and his army.

The American and French armies lined up in a large arc around the cornered British. The Redcoats hid behind defensive redoubts, but their backs were against the York River. Retreat was impossible if the coming battle did not go their way.

On September 28, the siege of Yorktown began. At first, there were minor skirmishes along the edges of the British defenses. By the beginning of October, George Washington punished the enemy with daily artillery barrages. The deadly cannon fire caused many enemy deaths. Lack of food and supplies also took their toll, and British morale sank.

As the siege wore on, Washington moved his troops and artillery closer and closer to the British defenders. On October 14, Captain Alexander Hamilton led a daring nighttime raid against a fortified British redoubt. French soldiers captured another British stronghold. Captured British cannons were turned on their former owners.

By October 17, 1781, the artillery bombardment and infantry assaults were too much for the British to bear. General Cornwallis sent an emissary to negotiate surrender terms with General Washington. The British had given up.

Patriot troops storm a British redoubt.

The British Army surrenders to the Patriots at Yorktown, Virginia, on October 19, 1781.

On October 19, 1781, the defeated Redcoats marched out of Yorktown and gave up their weapons to the victorious Patriot army and their French allies. General Cornwallis claimed he was too sick to personally surrender his army, so he sent his second in command in his place. George Washington refused to accept the ceremonial surrender sword. He had it given instead to his second in command, General Benjamin Lincoln.

At the end of the siege, the Americans lost 23 men killed and 65 wounded. The French lost 52 killed and 134 wounded. The British lost their entire army, with 156 killed, 326 wounded, and 7,157 taken prisoner.

Yorktown was the last big battle of the American Revolution. It highlighted the brilliant command of George Washington, and also the importance of America's French allies. When news of the defeat reached the ears of Great Britain's Prime Minister Lord Frederick North, he exclaimed, "Oh God! It is all over." The war would officially continue for two more years, but all major fighting ceased, and peace talks began at last.

THE TREATY OF PARIS

After General Cornwallis's disastrous loss at the Battle of Yorktown, the British Parliament demanded that peace be made with the United States. After years of war, the public could no longer stomach the tremendous cost in British blood and money. A pro-American majority came to power in Parliament, and King George III was forced to work with the opposition.

The American peace negotiators in Paris, France, from left to right: John Jay, John Adams, Benjamin Franklin, Henry Laurens, and secretary William Temple Franklin.

Peace talks began in April 1782, in Paris, France. At the beginning of the negotiations, the United States was represented by Benjamin Franklin. Franklin was later joined by John Jay, John Adams, and Henry Laurens. Richard Oswald represented Great Britain.

The peace talks progressed slowly. Great Britain was still fighting with France and Spain. The American Continental Congress also had to approve the final treaty, and the only way to communicate was by ship, which took weeks.

In the meantime, military skirmishes and raids continued in the United States, but they were small battles that didn't amount to much. For the most part, fighting in North America had ceased.

On September 3, 1783, the Treaty of Paris was finalized. Great Britain officially

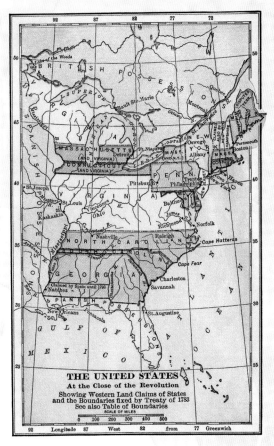

Borders of the United States in 1783.

recognized the independence of the United States. New boundaries were agreed upon (the Mississippi River was recognized as the United States's new western border), and all remaining British troops would be evacuated. At long last, the United States of America had won its freedom.

THE AFTERMATH OF WAR

The United States had won its freedom during the American Revolution, but it had come at a high cost. Many years of war took their toll both in destruction of property and blood spilled. Nobody knows exactly how many lives were lost in combat. Some estimate that as many as 25,000 Patriots died during military service. Those included about 8,000 deaths in battle. The rest were from wounds that festered, or from starvation and disease. During the winter of

Soldiers return home after the war.

1777–1778 alone, more than 2,500 soldiers died at winter camp at Valley Forge, Pennsylvania. Some historians think there were many more American military deaths, perhaps as many as 50,000. Because of poor or lost records, we may never know for sure.

On November 25, 1783, British soldiers began leaving New York City. George Washington and a group of loyal officers triumphantly rode through the streets on horseback to take possession of the long-suffering city.

General George Washington resigns as commander in chief of the Continental Army on December 23, 1783, at the Maryland State House in Annapolis.

In December, Washington resigned as commander in chief of the Continental Army. He then rode back to his beloved home at Mount Vernon, Virginia. This stunned the kings and queens of Europe, who expected Washington to use his power to become an American monarch.

Washington would later return to serve his country, first to help create a lasting Constitution, and then to serve as the nation's first president. It would take many years to rebuild the prosperity America enjoyed before the war, and to repay its debt. But the first order of business was to create a new and strong central government that would tie together the states into one, indivisible nation.

THE UNITED STATES CONSTITUTION

After the war, the shortcomings of the Articles of Confederation quickly came to the surface. The individual states had too much power. This made it very hard for the central government to do its job, like raise an army or regulate trade and taxes. Without a strong central government, it was next to impossible for the states to unite as one nation.

On September 17, 1787, members of the Constitutional Convention met in Philadelphia, Pennsylvania, to approve a new Constitution of the United States. More power was given to the central government.

The Constitution went into effect on March 4, 1789. Lawmakers, led by future president James Madison, soon created a set of 10 amendments, or changes, to the Constitution. Today we call these first 10 amendments the Bill of Rights. They protect individual freedoms, such as the right to free speech or the right to a fair trial.

The Constitution, while far from perfect, was an example to the world. The hard-fought American Revolution produced a new kind of government that protected the liberty and ideals of its citizens. Even today, the United States, and the ideas for which it stands, give hope to people everywhere.

TIMELINE

1778
Great Britain encourages Native Americans and British Loyalists to attack American settlers. Settlers retaliate in revenge attacks against Native Americans.

DECEMBER 1778
The British capture the river port town of Savannah, Georgia.

FEBRUARY 25, 1779
General George Rogers Clark and his frontiersmen militia take the British stronghold at Vincennes.

AUGUST 29, 1779
The Battle of Newtown is fought in New York. Patriots defeat a force of British Loyalists and their Iroquois allies.

APRIL AND MAY 1780
British forces capture Charleston, South Carolina, crushing the American Patriots.

AUGUST 16, 1780
The Battle of Camden, South Carolina, is another stunning loss for the Americans.

OCTOBER 7, 1780
The Battle of Kings Mountain, South Carolina, is a much-needed victory for the Americans.

JANUARY 17, 1781
The Battle of Cowpens is another American victory. Morale soars.

MARCH 1, 1781
The Articles of Confederation and Perpetual Union, the United States's first constitution, is approved and ratified.

MARCH 15, 1781
The Battle of Guilford Courthouse is won by British General Cornwallis, but at a terrible cost of hundreds of casualties.

SEPTEMBER 5, 1781
French ships severely damage seven British ships at Chesapeake Bay, preventing troops and supplies from reaching Cornwallis.

SEPTEMBER 28, 1781
The siege of Yorktown, Virginia, begins.

OCTOBER 19, 1781
British forces surrender to the American and French armies at the Battle of Yorktown.

SEPTEMBER 3, 1783
The Treaty of Paris is finalized. The United States is officially independent from Britain.

DECEMBER 23, 1783
Washington resigns as commander in chief of the Continental Army.

MARCH 4, 1789
The U.S. Constitution goes into effect. The hard-fought American Revolution produces a new kind of government that protects its citizens's liberties and ideals.

GLOSSARY

ARTILLERY

Large weapons of war, such as cannons, mortars, and howitzers, that are used by military forces on land and at sea.

BILL OF RIGHTS

The first 10 amendments to the United States Constitution. The Bill of Rights lists the special freedoms every human is born with and is able to enjoy in America. Also, the Bill of Rights tells the government that it cannot stop people from fully using and enjoying those freedoms unless the government has an extremely good reason for doing so.

CAVALRY

During the American Revolution era, soldiers who rode and fought on horseback were called cavalry. Modern cavalry includes soldiers who fight in armored vehicles such as tanks or attack helicopters.

CONTINENTAL CONGRESS

Lawmakers who governed the 13 colonies after they declared their independence from Great Britain.

GRAPESHOT

Round balls of lead or iron packed in a cloth bag.

GUERRILLA WARFARE

Warfare that is conducted by small groups of fighters (sometimes civilians instead of soldiers) who use the element of surprise and mobility to achieve their military objectives. Teams of guerrillas excel at ambushes and sabotage.

MILITIA

Citizens who were part-time soldiers rather than professional army fighters. Militiamen, such as the Minutemen from Massachusetts, usually fought only in their local areas and continued with their normal jobs when they were not needed.

MUSKET

A single-shot weapon, fired from the shoulder, that resembles a modern rifle. Muskets have smooth bores (the inside of the barrel). Their accuracy and range were limited, but a volley of muskets from a group of soldiers could be quite deadly.

PARLIAMENT

The law-making body of Great Britain. It consists of the House of Lords and the House of Commons.

PATRIOTS

Colonists who rebelled against Great Britain during the American Revolution.

REDCOATS

The name that was often given to British soldiers because part of their uniform included a bright red coat.

REDOUBT

A fort, or system of trenches and raised earthen berms. Redoubts are used to protect troops against frontal attacks. During the American Revolution they were temporary defensive structures often constructed of logs, piled dirt, or stones and bricks.

INDEX